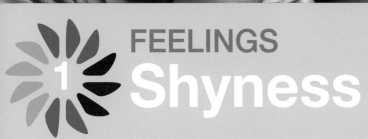

FEELINGS
1
Shyness

Tamra B. Orr

Published in the United States of America
by Cherry Lake Publishing
Ann Arbor, Michigan
www.cherrylakepublishing.com

Reading Adviser: Marla Conn MS, Ed., Literacy specialist, Read-Ability, Inc.

Photo Credits: © Brainsil/iStock Images, cover, 1; © Matthew Ennis/ Shutterstock Images, 4; © Dragon Images/ Shutterstock Images, 6; © Monkey Business Images/Shutterstock Images, 8; © Dmytro Zinkevych/Shutterstock Images, 10; © Dereje/Shutterstock Images, 12; © pedalist/Shutterstock Images, 14; © tomak/Shutterstock Images, 16; © Brenda Carson/Shutterstock Images, 18; © racorn/Shutterstock Images, 20

Library of Congress Cataloging-in-Publication Data
Names: Orr, Tamra, author.
    Title: Shyness / Tamra B. Orr.
Description: Ann Arbor : Cherry Lake Publishing, 2016. | Series: Feelings | Audience: K to Grade 3. | Includes bibliographical references and index.
Identifiers: LCCN 2015048118| ISBN 9781634710473 (hardcover) | ISBN 9781634711463 (pdf) | ISBN 9781634712453 (pbk.) | ISBN 9781634713443 (ebook)
Subjects: LCSH: Bashfulness—Juvenile literature.
Classification: LCC BF575.B3 O77 2016 | DDC 152.4—dc23
LC record available at http://lccn.loc.gov/2015048118

Cherry Lake Publishing would like to acknowledge the work of The Partnership for 21st Century Learning. Please visit *www.p21.org* for more information.

Printed in the United States of America
Corporate Graphics

Table of Contents

A Place to Hide

The **grocery store** is fun.

Mom picks out food I like.

We hold hands and sing silly songs.

Do these women look shy?

Uh-oh! Mom is talking to someone.

I need to hide.

Behind Mom's Legs

I duck behind Mom's legs where it's safe.

How can you tell this boy is shy?

I peek out at the lady talking to us.

She smiles at me. I close my eyes tight.

Say Hello?

Talking to new people is hard for me.

I know they are nice, but I feel **shy**.

When I feel shy, I do not know what to say.

My face feels hot and turns red.

A New Friend

Mom kneels down
next to me.

"This is our **neighbor**.
She is the one who makes
us cookies."

How is this girl feeling?

Oh! I remember those cookies.
I smile and **quietly** say, "Hello."

Find Out More

Berry, Joy. *Let's Talk About Being Shy*. Wheaton, IL: Watkins Publishing House, 2013.

Davies, Emma May, and Philip Watson. *Ellie the Shy Chick*. Philip Watson, 2015.

de Bezenac, Agnes, and Salem de Bezenac. *Tiny Thoughts on Shyness*. iCharacter, 2013.

Glossary

grocery store (GROH-sur-ee STOR) a store selling all types of food and drinks

neighbor (NAY-bur) a person who lives close to you

quietly (KWYE-it-lee) softly, not loudly

shy (SHYE) uncomfortable with others

Home and School Connection

Use this list of words from the book to help your child become a
better reader. Word games and writing activities can help
beginning readers reinforce literacy skills.

and	hard	not	smiles
are	hello	one	someone
behind	hide	our	songs
but	hold	out	store
close	hot	peek	talking
cookies	kneels	people	the
down	know	picks	they
duck	lady	quietly	this
eyes	legs	red	those
face	like	remember	tight
feel	makes	safe	turns
feels	mom	say	what
food	need	she	when
for	neighbor	shy	where
fun	new	silly	who
grocery	next	sing	
hands	nice	smile	

Index

About the Author

Tamra Orr has written more than 400 books for young people. The only thing she loves more than writing books is reading them. She lives in beautiful Portland, Oregon, with her husband, four children, dog, and cat. She says that she can remember being very shy long, long ago.